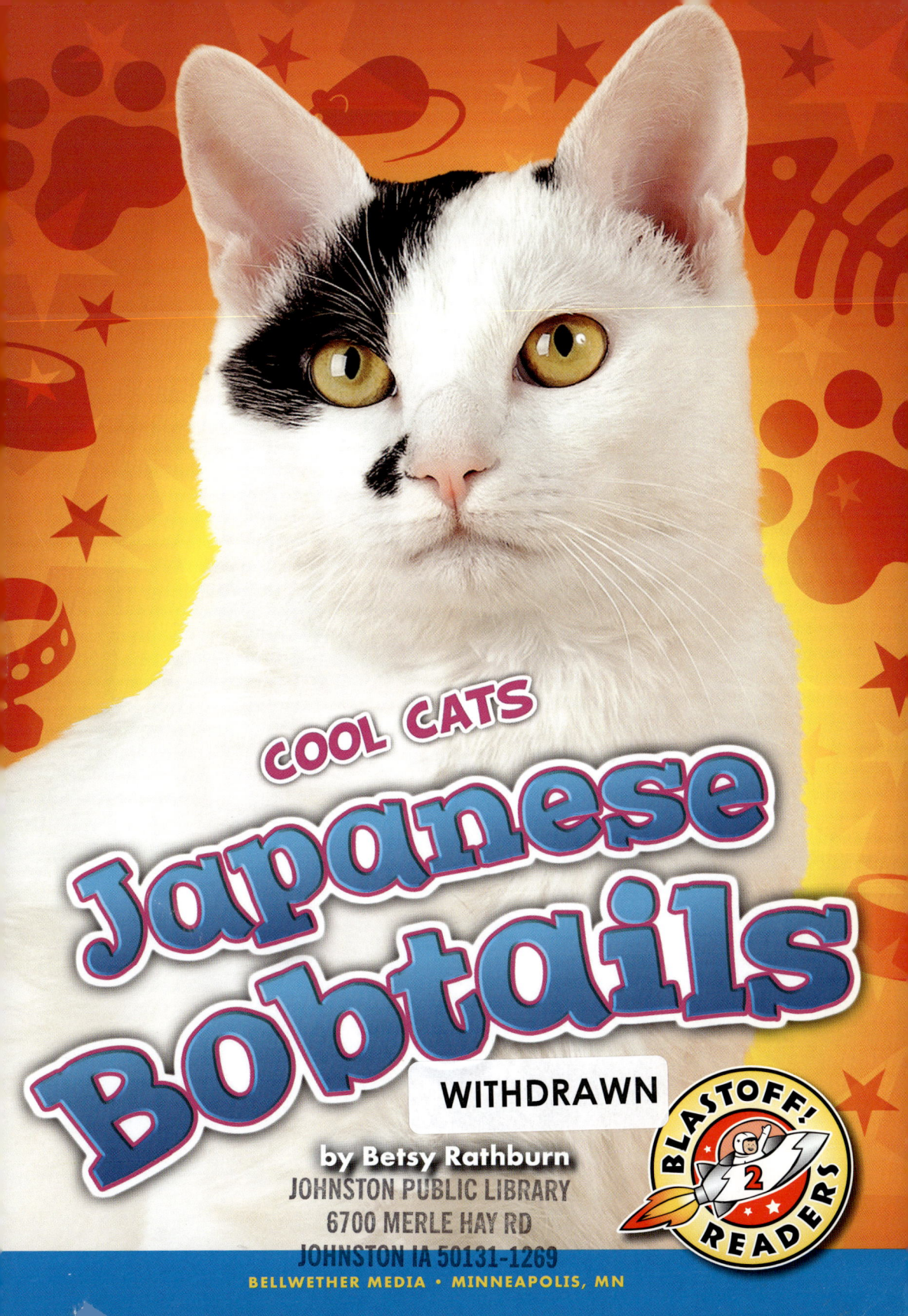

Note to Librarians, Teachers, and Parents:

Blastoff! Readers are carefully developed by literacy experts and combine standards-based content with developmentally appropriate text.

Level 1 provides the most support through repetition of high-frequency words, light text, predictable sentence patterns, and strong visual support.

Level 2 offers early readers a bit more challenge through varied simple sentences, increased text load, and less repetition of high-frequency words.

Level 3 advances early-fluent readers toward fluency through increased text and concept load, less reliance on visuals, longer sentences, and more literary language.

Level 4 builds reading stamina by providing more text per page, increased use of punctuation, greater variation in sentence patterns, and increasingly challenging vocabulary.

Level 5 encourages children to move from "learning to read" to "reading to learn" by providing even more text, varied writing styles, and less familiar topics.

Whichever book is right for your reader, Blastoff! Readers are the perfect books to build confidence and encourage a love of reading that will last a lifetime!

This edition first published in 2017 by Bellwether Media, Inc.

No part of this publication may be reproduced in whole or in part without written permission of the publisher. For information regarding permission, write to Bellwether Media, Inc., Attention: Permissions Department, 5357 Penn Avenue South, Minneapolis, MN 55419.

Library of Congress Cataloging-in-Publication Data

Names: Rathburn, Betsy, author.
Title: Japanese Bobtails / by Betsy Rathburn.
Other titles: Blastoff! Readers. 2, Cool Cats.
Description: Minneapolis, MN : Bellwether Media, Inc., 2017. | Series: Blastoff! Readers. Cool Cats | Audience: Ages 5-8. | Audience: K to grade 3. | Includes bibliographical references and index.
Identifiers: LCCN 2016032032 (print) | LCCN 2016042913 (ebook) | ISBN 9781626175624 (hardcover : alk. paper) | ISBN 9781681032832 (ebook)
Subjects: LCSH: Japanese bobtail cat–Juvenile literature.
Classification: LCC SF449.J37 R38 2017 (print) | LCC SF449.J37 (ebook) | DDC 636.8/22-dc23
LC record available at https://lccn.loc.gov/2016032032

Text copyright © 2017 by Bellwether Media, Inc. BLASTOFF! READERS and associated logos are trademarks and/or registered trademarks of Bellwether Media, Inc. SCHOLASTIC, CHILDREN'S PRESS, and associated logos are trademarks and/or registered trademarks of Scholastic Inc.

Editor: Christina Leaf   Designer: Lois Stanfield

Printed in the United States of America, North Mankato, MN.

Table of Contents

What Are Japanese Bobtails?	4
History of Japanese Bobtails	8
Short Tails and Big Ears	12
Smart Singers	18
Glossary	22
To Learn More	23
Index	24

What Are Japanese Bobtails?

Japanese bobtails are not like most cats. Their tails are short and fluffy.

People think their tails look like rabbit tails!

The cats can have long or short hair. Their **coats** are smooth and **silky**.

Some think Japanese bobtails bring good luck. People often place statues of them in their homes.

History of Japanese Bobtails

The first Japanese bobtails lived in Japan. **Centuries** of stories and art made them famous there.

These **mousers** kept rats away from scrolls in **temples**. They also protected silkworms in barns.

In 1968, Elizabeth Freret brought the **breed** to the United States. People loved its unusual appearance.

Today, people around the world own Japanese bobtails.

Short Tails and Big Ears

All Japanese bobtails are born with a short tail. Each tail is different.

They can be curvy or twisted. Some curl like pig tails!

tabby coat

The cats can have **solid** or patterned coats.

The *mi-ke*, or **calico**, pattern is popular. It is considered lucky in Japan.

Japanese bobtails have big ears that stick straight up. Their **slanted** eyes can be any color. Sometimes each eye is a different color!

Japanese Bobtail Profile

big ears

slanted eyes

triangle-shaped head

short, fluffy tail

Weight: 6 to 10 pounds (3 to 5 kilograms)

Life Span: 9 to 15 years

Smart Singers

Japanese bobtails are **intelligent**. They can learn to walk on a leash.

They are also **agile**. Some are taught to jump through hoops.

Japanese bobtails are singers. They love to chirp and meow.

People love these **vocal** cats!

Glossary

agile—able to move quickly and easily

breed—a type of cat

calico—a pattern that has patches of white, black, and reddish brown fur

centuries—hundreds of years

coats—the hair or fur covering some animals

intelligent—able to learn and be trained

mousers—cats that catch mice

silky—soft, smooth, and shiny

slanted—at an angle

solid—one color

temples—religious buildings

vocal—expressing sound often or loudly

To Learn More

AT THE LIBRARY

Henrichs, Wendy. *I Am Tama, Lucky Cat: A Japanese Legend.* Atlanta, Ga.: Peachtree, 2011.

Sexton, Colleen. *The Life Cycle of a Cat.* Minneapolis, Minn.: Bellwether Media, 2011.

Wheeler, Jill C. *Japanese Bobtail Cats.* Minneapolis, Minn.: ABDO Pub Co., 2012.

ON THE WEB

Learning more about Japanese bobtails is as easy as 1, 2, 3.

1. Go to www.factsurfer.com.

2. Enter "Japanese bobtails" into the search box.

3. Click the "Surf" button and you will see a list of related web sites.

With factsurfer.com, finding more information is just a click away.

Index

art, 8
barns, 9
breed, 10
chirp, 20
coats, 6, 14, 15
colors, 14
ears, 16, 17
eyes, 16, 17
Freret, Elizabeth, 10
hoops, 19
Japan, 8, 15
jump, 19
learn, 18
leash, 18
life span, 17
luck, 7, 15
meow, 20
mousers, 9
patterns, 14, 15
rats, 9

scrolls, 9
silkworms, 9
singers, 20
size, 17
statues, 7
stories, 8
tails, 4, 5, 12, 13, 17
temples, 9
United States, 10
vocal, 21

The images in this book are reproduced through the courtesy of: dien, front cover, p. 6; Gerard Lacz Images/ VW Pics/ Zuma Press, pp. 4-5; Jean-Michel Labat/ ardea.com/ SuperStock, pp. 5, 8, 15 (upper right); Utt4659, p. 7; Robin Burkett/ Animal-Photography, pp. 9, 18; Juniors/ Juniors/ SuperStock, pp. 10, 14-15, 15 (lower right), 21; Christian Science Monitor/ Getty, p. 11; Gerard Lacz/ SuperStock, p. 12; Alan Robinson/ Animal-Photography, pp. 12-13 (cat), 15 (lower left), 17; pepoja, pp. 12-13 (background); Dmitri Pravdjukov, pp. 15 (upper left), 20 (cat); Helmi Flick/ Animal-Photography, pp. 16-17 (cat); Alexandre Zveiger, pp. 16-17 (background); Mario Tama/ Getty, p. 19; Seregraff, p. 20 (mouth).